# Baby the Vampire Terrier's Christmas Adventure

# Baby the Vampire Terrier's Christmas Adventure

Matthew Petchinsky

# Baby the Vampire Terrier's Christmas Adventure
By: Matthew Petchinsky

## Introduction

The small, enchanting town of Moonlit Hollow nestled beneath a canopy of snow-dusted pines has always been a magical place. With its cobblestone streets illuminated by the soft glow of old-fashioned lanterns, the town feels like something out of a storybook, especially during Christmastime. Wreaths adorned with sparkling ornaments and crimson bows hang from every doorway, and the air is alive with the sweet aroma of spiced cider, freshly baked gingerbread, and the ever-so-slight tingle of snowflakes yet to fall.

For the residents of Moonlit Hollow, Christmas isn't just a holiday—it's a season of unity, joy, and, of course, a touch of magic. From the annual tree-lighting ceremony in the town square to the festive caroling that echoes through the crisp night air, everyone takes part in spreading cheer. However, there's one resident who looks forward to Christmas more than anyone else: Baby the Vampire Terrier.

Baby may be small, with her glossy black coat and twinkling crimson eyes, but she has a big heart—and an even bigger love for the holiday season. To her, Christmas is more than twinkling lights and beautifully wrapped presents; it's about kindness, togetherness, and the thrill of a great adventure. And Moonlit Hollow always seems to deliver just that.

But this year, as the town buzzes with holiday preparations, something feels... off. At first, it's just little things—decorations mysteriously vanishing from the town square, the sound of distant, eerie laughter echoing through the forest, and a chill in the air that seems to bite harder than usual. Baby's keen vampire senses can pick up on the unease. Something is amiss, and as the days grow shorter and Christmas draws closer, the strange happenings become harder to ignore.

Baby isn't one to sit idly by when her beloved town is in trouble. With her trusty companions—a clever crow named Midnight, the ever-curious fairy Pixie, and a wise old cat named Professor Whiskerby—Baby sets out to investigate. Together, they form an unlikely but formidable team, each bringing their unique talents and perspectives to the mystery at hand.

Their journey takes them through Moonlit Hollow's most iconic locations: the bustling Christmas Market with its twinkling stalls, the serene and snow-covered Whispering Woods, and even the eerie ruins of the old Sugarplum Factory, long abandoned but rumored to hold secrets of its own. Along the way, they uncover a sinister plot that threatens not only the festive season but the very spirit of Christmas itself.

As Baby and her friends dig deeper, they face challenges that test their courage, resourcefulness, and the strength of their bond. It's not just about saving decorations or stopping mischief-makers; it's about protecting the magic that makes Christmas so special—something Moonlit Hollow and its residents hold dear.

This heartwarming tale of friendship, bravery, and the power of Christmas spirit will transport you to a world where even the unlikeliest heroes can make a difference. So, bundle up, grab a cup of cocoa, and get ready to join Baby the Vampire Terrier on a holiday adventure like no other. Moonlit Hollow is waiting, and Christmas needs saving!

## Chapter 1: The Missing Christmas Lights

The snow had just begun to fall softly over Moonlit Hollow, draping the town in a blanket of glistening white. Twinkling Christmas lights adorned every house, turning the cobblestone streets into a magical kaleidoscope of color. Baby the Vampire Terrier, perched on the windowsill of her cozy cottage, gazed out with sparkling excitement in her crimson eyes. Christmas was her favorite time of year, and Moonlit Hollow was at its most enchanting during the holiday season.

But something wasn't quite right.

Baby's sharp vampire senses tingled, a faint feeling that something was amiss. Her nose twitched, and her ears perked up as she scanned the houses down the street. It wasn't the usual hustle and bustle of holiday cheer that caught her attention—it was the absence of it.

"Pip!" Baby called, her voice carrying a blend of urgency and curiosity.

A moment later, Pip the bat fluttered into the room. With his oversized wings and endearing round eyes, he was Baby's closest companion and her most trusted sidekick. Pip landed gracefully on the edge of the windowsill, his tiny claws gripping the wood as he peered out into the night.

"What's wrong, Baby?" Pip asked, his high-pitched voice laced with concern.

Baby pointed with her paw toward the row of houses across the street. "Look! The Christmas lights are gone! The Garlands had their house lit up just last night, and now it's completely dark."

Pip squinted, his keen bat vision scanning the houses. "You're right," he said, tilting his head. "And it's not just their house. The Evergreens' lights are missing too!"

Baby leapt down from the windowsill, her little paws making soft thuds against the wooden floor. "This isn't normal. People in Moonlit

Hollow take their Christmas decorations seriously. Something's happening, and we're going to find out what."

Without hesitation, Baby grabbed her tiny red scarf, wrapping it snugly around her neck. Pip perched on her shoulder as they set off into the chilly night. The streets of Moonlit Hollow were eerily quiet, the usual festive glow dimmed by the absence of lights. Only the faint hum of the town's main Christmas tree in the square remained, casting long shadows that danced in the moonlight.

As Baby and Pip made their way down the street, they stopped at the Garlands' house. The family had been known for their extravagant holiday displays—strings of lights in every color, glowing reindeer on the lawn, and a giant inflatable Santa waving to passersby. But now, the house sat in total darkness, the decorations vanished without a trace.

"Let's see if anyone's home," Baby said, hopping up to the front door. She gave three sharp barks, her way of knocking. After a few moments, Mrs. Garland opened the door, her face pale and worried.

"Baby! Oh, thank goodness you're here," Mrs. Garland exclaimed. "Our lights are gone! We woke up this morning, and everything was just... gone. It's like they disappeared into thin air."

"Did you hear or see anything unusual last night?" Baby asked, her voice calm but determined.

Mrs. Garland shook her head. "No, nothing. We went to bed, and everything was perfectly fine. But when we woke up, the decorations were gone, and the wires were cut. It's as if someone—or something—stole them."

Baby exchanged a glance with Pip. "Don't worry, Mrs. Garland. We'll get to the bottom of this."

As they continued their investigation, Baby and Pip visited several more houses, all with the same story: decorations and lights stolen in the dead of night, leaving no clues except for faint traces of footprints in the snow that disappeared near the edge of the Whispering Woods.

"The Whispering Woods," Pip said, shivering slightly. "Do you think...?"

Baby's eyes narrowed. "It's too early to say for sure, but it's definitely suspicious. We need to follow the trail."

The duo padded silently through the streets until they reached the edge of the forest. The trees stood tall and foreboding, their branches bare and skeletal against the pale moonlight. The footprints Baby had been following stopped abruptly, as if the culprit had vanished into thin air.

"Whoever—or whatever—did this is trying to hide," Baby murmured. "But they can't hide from us."

Pip flapped his wings, hovering above Baby's head. "Should we go in now or wait until morning?"

Baby considered this for a moment. The Whispering Woods were known for their peculiar enchantments and occasional tricks of light. Venturing in at night was risky, but time was of the essence.

"We go now," Baby decided. "If someone's trying to ruin Christmas, we can't waste another moment."

With Pip at her side, Baby took her first cautious steps into the forest. The air grew colder, and the faint scent of pine mixed with something metallic and unfamiliar. In the distance, a faint flicker of light caught their attention—a glow that seemed to dance and shimmer like the stolen Christmas lights.

"Do you see that?" Pip whispered, his voice barely audible.

Baby nodded. "I do. And I think we've just found our first clue."

Together, they moved deeper into the woods, the mystery of the missing Christmas lights pulling them further into the unknown. Whatever lay ahead, Baby knew one thing for certain: she wouldn't stop until the lights—and Christmas—were restored to Moonlit Hollow.

## Chapter 2: The Frosty Clue

The Whispering Woods stood in haunting silence, its skeletal branches creaking softly under the weight of the snow. A faint glow lingered deep within the forest, teasing the edges of Baby's vision like a flickering beacon. She had never been one to back down from a mystery, especially when Christmas itself was at stake. Beside her, Pip the bat perched on a low-hanging branch, his wings folded tightly against his body.

"Do you feel that, Baby?" Pip whispered. "It's colder here—colder than it should be."

Baby sniffed the frosty air, her sharp vampire senses detecting an unusual chill that seemed to hum with an otherworldly energy. It wasn't the ordinary nip of winter. This was something different—something unnatural. Her crimson eyes narrowed as her keen nose picked up another clue.

"Over here!" Baby barked softly, motioning Pip to follow.

In the freshly fallen snow, a trail of paw prints shimmered faintly, as though outlined in frost. The prints were larger than any dog's she had seen, with an unusual clawed pattern that hinted at something other than an ordinary animal. Most striking of all was the faint icy glow emanating from them, as though they were etched with the cold itself.

Pip fluttered down to inspect the tracks. "Those aren't normal paw prints," he said, his voice trembling slightly. "What kind of creature leaves glowing footprints?"

Baby crouched low to the ground, examining the prints closely. "Whatever it is, it's connected to the missing Christmas lights. Look here—tiny fragments of wire frozen into the snow."

Pip leaned in, his keen eyes spotting the thin metallic strands caught in the frost. "It must have dragged the lights through here," he said. "But why would it take them? And where is it going?"

Baby didn't have an answer, but her determination only deepened. "There's only one way to find out. We follow the trail."

With Pip flying just above her, Baby began tracking the paw prints deeper into the forest. The further they went, the colder the air became, until it felt like the very warmth of the world was being siphoned away. The soft crunch of snow under Baby's paws was the only sound, broken occasionally by the faint rustling of Pip's wings.

The prints led them to a clearing where the moonlight filtered through the bare branches, casting long shadows on the ground. In the center of the clearing stood a curious sight: a single, enormous snow-drift shaped unnaturally, as though sculpted by careful hands. It glowed faintly with the same icy energy as the paw prints.

"Stay close, Pip," Baby warned, her voice a low growl.

As they approached the snowdrift, Baby noticed something unusual: embedded within the frozen mound were fragments of stolen decorations. A strand of Christmas lights snaked through the snow, its bulbs dimmed but intact. Pieces of tinsel and ornaments peeked out from the icy surface, their vibrant colors muted by frost.

"What is this?" Pip murmured, hovering beside Baby. "It's like a hoard... but why?"

Baby's nose twitched as she sniffed the air. The metallic scent she'd noticed earlier was stronger here, mixed with the unmistakable aroma of pine and... something else. It was faint but distinct, a sharp, biting scent that made her fur bristle.

"This isn't just a snowdrift," Baby said, her voice steady but tinged with caution. "It's a hiding place. Whatever took the lights is storing them here."

Before Pip could respond, a sudden sound shattered the stillness of the forest—a low, rumbling growl that seemed to reverberate through the trees. Baby and Pip froze, their eyes darting toward the source of the noise. From the shadows at the edge of the clearing, two glowing blue eyes emerged, piercing through the darkness like shards of ice.

The creature stepped into the moonlight, revealing itself in full. It was unlike anything Baby had ever seen. Standing as tall as a wolf but with a more slender, sinewy frame, the creature's fur was pure white, shimmering as though dusted with snowflakes. Its claws were long and sharp, and its breath emerged in visible puffs, frosting the air around it. Most striking of all was the faint, ghostly glow that radiated from its body, the same icy energy that marked the paw prints.

Pip let out a squeak of alarm. "What is that?!"

Baby's eyes locked onto the creature, her body tensing in readiness. "I don't know," she admitted, "but it's guarding the lights."

The creature let out another growl, this one louder and more menacing, as it stepped protectively in front of the snowdrift. Baby stood her ground, her instincts telling her that this was no ordinary animal—it was something magical, something tied to the strange happenings in Moonlit Hollow.

"Easy," Baby said, her voice calm but firm. "We're not here to hurt you. We just want to know why you're taking the decorations."

The creature tilted its head, its glowing eyes narrowing as if it understood her words. For a moment, the tension in the air seemed to ease. But then, with a sudden burst of speed, it lunged toward Baby, its claws gleaming in the moonlight.

"Watch out!" Pip cried, swooping down to distract the creature.

Baby leapt to the side, her quick reflexes saving her from the creature's swipe. She landed gracefully in the snow, her eyes blazing with determination. "If you want to play, then let's play," she growled.

Pip darted around the creature's head, flapping his wings to draw its attention. "Baby, the lights!" he called. "It's protecting them for a reason. Maybe it's not trying to hurt Christmas—it might be trying to save something!"

Baby dodged another lunge, her mind racing. Pip's words made sense. The creature wasn't attacking recklessly; it was deliberate, defensive. There was more to this mystery than met the eye.

"Pip, keep it busy!" Baby shouted as she darted toward the snowdrift. Her sharp claws dug into the icy mound, pulling at the tangled strands of lights and decorations.

As she worked, the creature let out a mournful howl that sent chills down her spine. It wasn't a sound of rage—it was a sound of sorrow. Baby paused, her claws hovering over the lights.

"It's not trying to ruin Christmas," she realized aloud. "It's protecting something."

Pip, still dodging the creature's swipes, called out, "What do you mean?"

"I don't know yet," Baby replied, her voice steady. "But we're going to find out."

With the trail of icy paw prints and the mysterious snow creature, Baby knew this was only the beginning of a deeper mystery—one that could change the fate of Christmas in Moonlit Hollow forever.

## Chapter 3: Max and the Frost Goblins

The Whispering Woods were still and silent after the encounter with the glowing snow creature. Baby and Pip had retreated to a safe distance, their breaths visible in the biting cold air. Though the immediate threat had passed, the mystery had only deepened. What was the creature guarding? Why was it hoarding Christmas decorations? And more importantly, how did it tie into the strange events around Moonlit Hollow?

As Baby pondered their next move, a familiar sound broke the silence—a faint rustling in the underbrush, followed by a series of soft, excited yips.

"Max!" Pip exclaimed, flapping his wings excitedly.

From the shadows emerged Max, the werewolf puppy, his scruffy gray fur dusted with snow. His bright amber eyes glowed with excitement as he bounded toward them, his tail wagging furiously. Despite his fearsome lineage, Max was as playful and loyal as any ordinary pup—and a trusted friend of Baby and Pip.

"Baby! Pip!" Max barked, skidding to a stop in front of them. "I've been looking for you everywhere! Have you seen them yet?"

"Seen what?" Baby asked, tilting her head.

"The frost goblins!" Max exclaimed, his voice a mixture of excitement and worry. "They're everywhere! They've been sneaking into town, stealing decorations, and causing all sorts of trouble."

Baby's ears perked up at the mention of frost goblins. "So that's what's behind all of this," she murmured, her mind racing. "We thought it might be one creature, but this changes everything. How do you know it's frost goblins?"

Max sat down, his tail swishing through the snow as he spoke. "I saw them! They're small, quick, and covered in frost. They travel in packs and leave trails of icy footprints wherever they go. They're sneaky too—almost impossible to catch unless you know their tricks."

Pip flapped his wings nervously. "Why would they be stealing Christmas decorations?"

Max lowered his voice, leaning in as if sharing a secret. "Frost goblins don't like Christmas. They think the holiday's warmth and cheer melt their icy magic. They've been stealing decorations to dim the holiday spirit and strengthen their powers."

Baby frowned, her crimson eyes narrowing in determination. "Then we can't let them succeed. If the goblins want to take away Christmas, we'll have to stop them."

Max wagged his tail enthusiastically. "I knew you'd say that! That's why I came looking for you. I need your help. They've set up a hideout deeper in the woods—it's where they're keeping everything they've stolen."

Pip hovered closer, his curiosity piqued. "A hideout? How do you know where it is?"

Max grinned, his sharp puppy teeth gleaming. "I may have followed them last night. They didn't see me—I'm great at sneaking. I even heard them talking about their plans. They're gathering all the decorations to build some kind of icy fortress. They think it'll make them invincible."

Baby stood tall, her small frame radiating determination. "Then we don't have a moment to lose. Show us the way, Max."

The trio set off, Max leading the way through the forest. The trail was winding and treacherous, the snow growing deeper and the air colder with every step. Max's keen nose guided them through the maze of trees, while Baby's sharp eyes scanned for any sign of danger. Pip, ever watchful, flitted above them, keeping a lookout for any approaching goblins.

As they neared the hideout, the forest began to change. The trees were coated in a thick layer of frost, their branches glittering like shards of ice. The ground was hard and slick, and the air hummed with a strange, magical energy. Baby could feel it in her bones—a chill that wasn't just from the cold.

"There," Max whispered, nodding toward a cluster of icy spires that jutted out from the ground like frozen teeth. The spires formed a jagged ring around a central clearing, where the goblins' hideout lay.

Baby crouched low, her crimson eyes narrowing as she surveyed the scene. The frost goblins were exactly as Max had described—small, wiry creatures with sharp, angular features and skin that glimmered like frost. Their eyes glowed an eerie blue, and they moved with a quick, skittering gait, their clawed hands carrying stolen decorations into the hideout.

The hideout itself was a strange, otherworldly structure. It resembled an ice castle, with walls made of frozen shards and towers that sparkled in the moonlight. Strands of Christmas lights hung from the spires, their bulbs dimmed but still recognizable. Ornaments, garlands, and even entire wreaths were embedded in the icy walls, creating a bizarre and unsettling display.

Pip shivered. "What do we do now? There are so many of them."

Baby's mind worked quickly. "We need a plan. If we rush in, they'll scatter, and we'll lose our chance to recover the decorations."

Max's tail wagged thoughtfully. "I can create a distraction. Frost goblins hate noise, and I'm great at making a ruckus."

Baby nodded. "That could work. While you distract them, Pip and I will sneak into the hideout and figure out how to recover the decorations. If we can find their leader, we might be able to stop this for good."

Max's eyes gleamed with excitement. "Leave it to me!"

As Max bounded off to prepare his distraction, Baby and Pip crept closer to the hideout, their movements silent and precise. The frost goblins chattered among themselves in a strange, tinkling language, oblivious to the approaching danger.

"Are you ready, Pip?" Baby whispered.

Pip nodded, his tiny claws clutching the edge of her scarf. "Ready as I'll ever be."

With their plan in motion, Baby and her friends were determined to face the frost goblins head-on. The stakes were high, but their resolve was unshakable. Christmas wasn't just a holiday—it was a symbol of hope and joy. And Baby wasn't about to let the frost goblins take that away from Moonlit Hollow.

**Chapter 4: A Vampire Terrier's Sleigh Ride**

The icy glow of the frost goblins' hideout faded into the distance as Baby and Pip regrouped with Max. The werewolf puppy's distraction had worked brilliantly, scattering the goblins and giving Baby and Pip a chance to survey the situation. But with the decorations still locked away in their icy fortress, the trio needed a new plan to save Christmas.

It was then that a faint jingling sound caught Baby's sharp ears, growing louder with every passing second. She perked up, her crimson eyes scanning the frosty woods. The sound was unmistakable—bells, bright and merry, carried on the crisp night air.

"Do you hear that?" Pip whispered, his wings twitching.

"Bells," Baby said, her voice steady but curious. "And they're getting closer."

Max sniffed the air, his nose twitching excitedly. "I smell reindeer! And... cookies?"

Before Baby could respond, a blur of red and gold streaked through the trees, heading straight toward them. As it drew closer, Baby could make out the shape of a miniature sleigh, pulled by four tiny reindeer no bigger than fawns. The sleigh was piled high with presents, its golden runners gliding effortlessly over the snow. The jingling bells hung from the reindeer's harnesses, their sound as cheerful as the season itself.

But something wasn't right. The sleigh wobbled precariously, and the reindeer seemed panicked, their eyes wide with fear. Behind them, a group of frost goblins gave chase, their icy claws outstretched as they cackled and hissed.

"They're trying to steal the sleigh!" Pip exclaimed.

Baby's eyes narrowed. "Not on my watch."

Without a second thought, Baby sprang into action. Her vampire speed kicked in, her small body a blur as she darted through the snow. Pip flew alongside her, struggling to keep up with her swift, determined pace.

"Max, stay here!" Baby called over her shoulder. "We'll handle this."

Max barked in protest but knew better than to argue. He watched as Baby closed the distance between herself and the sleigh, her paws barely touching the ground. The frost goblins were gaining on the reindeer, their clawed feet skittering across the ice with unnatural speed.

With a burst of energy, Baby leapt into the air, landing gracefully on the back of the sleigh. The reindeer let out frightened snorts, their tiny hooves pounding against the snow as they raced forward.

"Whoa, easy there," Baby said, her voice soothing but firm. She took hold of the sleigh's reins, her small paws steady despite the chaos. "You're safe now."

The goblins screeched in frustration, their icy claws swiping at the sleigh. One particularly bold goblin lunged, grabbing hold of the back edge. Baby turned, her fangs gleaming as she let out a warning growl.

"Get off!" she barked, swiping at the goblin with her claws.

The goblin hissed but lost its grip, tumbling into the snow as the sleigh sped away. The others gave up the chase, their angry cries fading into the distance. Baby glanced back, ensuring the goblins were no longer a threat before turning her attention to the reindeer.

"Good job, everyone," she said, her tone reassuring. "You're safe now."

The reindeer slowed to a stop, their breaths visible in the cold air. Pip fluttered down, landing on the edge of the sleigh. "That was amazing, Baby! But why were the goblins after this sleigh?"

Baby's keen eyes scanned the sleigh's contents. The presents were wrapped in shimmering paper, each adorned with a tag that read, *"From Santa Claus."* Beneath the gifts, something caught her attention—a scroll tied with a crimson ribbon, partially hidden beneath the golden seat.

"What's this?" Baby murmured, pulling the scroll free.

She unrolled it carefully, revealing a detailed map of Moonlit Hollow. Several locations were marked with red X's, including the town square, the Whispering Woods, and a spot deep within the forest labeled *"Frost Goblin Lair."*

"This is it!" Baby exclaimed, her crimson eyes gleaming with excitement. "This map shows us exactly where their main hideout is."

Pip peered over her shoulder. "But why would they have this? And why were they trying to steal Santa's sleigh?"

Baby's expression grew serious. "I think the goblins are planning something bigger than just stealing decorations. They're targeting Santa now. If they capture him or his sleigh, they could ruin Christmas for the entire world."

Pip shuddered. "We can't let that happen."

Baby nodded. "We won't. First, we need to get this sleigh back to safety. Then, we'll use this map to find their lair and put an end to their plans."

Taking the reins once more, Baby guided the reindeer through the forest, her small but capable paws steady on the golden handles. The sleigh glided smoothly over the snow, its bells jingling softly as the night began to quiet. Pip kept watch, his sharp eyes scanning the trees for any sign of danger.

As they neared the edge of the woods, Baby felt a renewed sense of purpose. The map in her possession was the key to solving the mystery and saving Christmas. But she also knew that the frost goblins wouldn't give up without a fight.

"Pip," she said, her voice firm but calm, "this is just the beginning. We're going to need all the help we can get."

Pip nodded, his tiny claws gripping the edge of the sleigh. "Whatever it takes, Baby. We'll stop them."

With the sleigh safely in tow and a vital clue in their possession, Baby and Pip prepared for the next chapter of their adventure. The frost goblins might have been clever, but they hadn't counted on the determination of a vampire terrier and her friends. Christmas wasn't just a holiday to Baby—it was a promise of hope, magic, and togetherness. And she was ready to fight for it.

## Chapter 5: The Enchanted Gingerbread House

The dense trees of the Whispering Woods thinned as Baby, Pip, and Max followed the map deeper into the forest. The air was colder here, carrying a sweet, almost intoxicating scent of cinnamon, nutmeg, and sugar. Baby sniffed the air, her crimson eyes narrowing as the aroma grew stronger.

"We're close," she said, her voice steady but tinged with caution.

Pip fluttered above her, his wings carrying him just high enough to scout ahead. "That smell... it's like cookies. But it's so strong it almost makes me dizzy."

Max's tail wagged as he bounded beside Baby, his nose to the ground. "It's coming from over there," he said, pointing his paw toward a clearing just ahead. "But it smells weird—too sweet, like it's trying to trick us."

As they stepped into the clearing, the source of the scent came into view. Standing in the middle of the frosted clearing was an enormous gingerbread house. It looked like something out of a fairy tale, with walls made of golden-brown gingerbread, a roof tiled with colorful gumdrops, and frosted shingles glistening in the moonlight. Candy canes framed the doorway, and sparkling sugar coated the windows like panes of frosty glass.

But there was something off about the house. The candy seemed to shimmer unnaturally, and the glow from the windows wasn't warm or inviting—it was cold and eerie, casting long, unnatural shadows on the snow. Around the house, frost goblins scurried back and forth, carrying stolen decorations and supplies into the structure. Their high-pitched chatter echoed through the clearing as they worked, their sharp claws clicking against the icy ground.

"An enchanted gingerbread house," Baby murmured. "It's perfect for them—sweet on the outside, but dangerous underneath."

Max growled softly, his hackles rising. "How are we supposed to get in? They'll see us coming from a mile away."

Pip hovered close to Baby, his voice a nervous whisper. "Maybe we should wait for them to leave."

Baby shook her head. "We don't have time. If the goblins are planning to use this house as their base, we need to act now. But we can't fight them head-on—not yet."

Her sharp mind worked quickly, formulating a plan. "I'll go in alone," she said. "I'm small enough to sneak inside without being noticed. Max, you and Pip stay out here and keep watch. If anything happens, make a distraction to draw them away."

Max's ears drooped. "Are you sure, Baby? What if you get caught?"

Baby gave him a reassuring smile. "Don't worry about me. I've dealt with worse than frost goblins. Just be ready."

With that, Baby crept forward, her small frame blending seamlessly with the shadows. She moved silently, her vampire speed allowing her to dart between cover with ease. As she approached the gingerbread house, she noticed more details: the gumdrops on the roof glimmered like crystals, and the candy canes framing the doorway had a faint, magical aura. Even the snow around the house sparkled unnaturally, as if it had been dusted with enchanted sugar.

Baby crouched low, her keen eyes scanning for an opening. She spotted a small crack near the base of the house where a piece of gingerbread had crumbled away. It was just big enough for her to squeeze through. Carefully, she wriggled inside, her nose twitching as the sweet scent grew overpowering.

The interior of the house was just as strange as the exterior. The walls were lined with more stolen decorations, glittering ornaments and strands of lights embedded in the gingerbread like trophies. The floor was sticky with syrup, and the air was thick with a magical chill. At the center of the room stood a towering cauldron, bubbling with a shimmering blue liquid that radiated cold. Around it, frost goblins bustled about, adding ingredients to the brew and muttering in their tinkling, eerie language.

Baby pressed herself against the wall, her small body hidden in the shadows. Her crimson eyes scanned the room, taking in every detail. She noticed a pile of presents near the cauldron, their tags reading *"From Santa Claus."* Her heart sank. The goblins weren't just stealing decorations—they were stealing gifts meant for children all over the world.

"I have to stop this," Baby thought, her determination hardening.

But first, she needed more information. Quietly, she crept closer to the goblins, her ears straining to catch their conversation. Though their language was strange, she could pick out a few words.

"Fortress... complete... Christmas spirit... destroy."

Baby's mind raced. The goblins weren't just hoarding decorations—they were using them to drain the magic of Christmas itself. The cauldron was the key, its icy brew designed to sap the warmth and joy from the holiday.

Before she could process further, a loud crack echoed through the room as a goblin accidentally dropped a candy cane staff. The sound startled another goblin, who turned and caught a glimpse of Baby's reflection in a shiny ornament.

"INTRUDER!" the goblin screeched, its voice piercing and shrill.

Baby's heart leapt as the room erupted into chaos. Goblins scrambled toward her, their icy claws outstretched. Thinking quickly, Baby darted toward the pile of presents, using her speed and agility to stay ahead of her pursuers. She grabbed a small silver box from the pile, sensing it was important, and tucked it under her scarf.

"Max! Pip! Distraction, now!" she barked, her voice echoing through the house.

Outside, Max howled, his mournful cry sending a ripple of unease through the goblins. Pip swooped down from the trees, knocking over a pile of candy canes near the entrance and sending them scattering like bowling pins. The goblins rushed to the windows, momentarily distracted by the commotion outside.

Seizing the opportunity, Baby bolted for the crack in the wall. She squeezed through just as the goblins realized what was happening, their angry cries ringing out behind her. Max and Pip were already waiting, their eyes wide with relief as she emerged.

"Run!" Baby shouted, clutching the silver box tightly as they fled into the forest.

The goblins didn't give chase, too wary of venturing far from their enchanted lair. As the trio put distance between themselves and the gingerbread house, Baby glanced down at the box she had taken. It was small and unassuming, but it radiated a faint, warm energy—a stark contrast to the icy magic of the goblins.

"What's in it?" Pip asked, his wings fluttering with curiosity.

Baby shook her head. "I don't know yet, but it's important. I can feel it."

Max sniffed the box, his tail wagging nervously. "It smells like... hope."

Baby's eyes glimmered with determination. "Whatever it is, it's the key to stopping the goblins. We just have to figure out how to use it."

With the enchanted gingerbread house behind them and a mysterious new clue in hand, Baby, Pip, and Max pressed on. The goblins might have the upper hand for now, but the tide was turning. Christmas wasn't lost—not yet. And Baby wasn't about to let the magic of the season slip away.

## Chapter 6: The Goblins' Snowy Plan

The moon hung high over the Whispering Woods, its pale light casting long shadows across the frozen landscape. Baby, Pip, and Max had taken refuge in a hollowed-out tree not far from the enchanted gingerbread house. The silver box Baby had stolen from the goblins sat between them, radiating a faint warmth that seemed to cut through the biting chill of the night.

"We need to know what's inside," Pip said, his wings twitching nervously. "If it's important enough for the goblins to keep near their cauldron, it might be the key to stopping them."

Baby's crimson eyes narrowed as she studied the box. "I don't want to risk opening it here. If it's enchanted, it could alert the goblins. We need to focus on gathering more information first."

Max, who had been sniffing the air, suddenly perked up. His ears swiveled toward the gingerbread house, his amber eyes narrowing. "They're talking," he whispered. "I can hear them."

Baby's sharp ears picked up the faint, high-pitched chatter of the frost goblins. She gestured for Pip and Max to stay quiet as she crept to the edge of the hollow tree. The goblins' voices carried on the icy wind, their strange, tinkling language filled with urgency. Baby crouched low, her senses honed, as she translated their words in her mind.

"...the cauldron is ready... freeze the town... no warmth, no Christmas."

Her heart sank. The frost goblins weren't content with stealing decorations and gifts—they were planning something far worse. They intended to freeze the entire town of Moonlit Hollow, plunging it into an eternal winter where no holiday cheer could survive.

Baby turned back to Pip and Max, her voice low but firm. "They're planning to freeze Moonlit Hollow. If they succeed, Christmas will be lost forever."

Max growled softly, his fur bristling. "How are they going to do it?"

"They're using the cauldron in the gingerbread house," Baby explained. "It's filled with some kind of icy magic. If they activate it, the magic will spread across the town, freezing everything in its path."

Pip fluttered nervously, his tiny claws gripping the edge of the hollow. "We have to stop them! But how? That cauldron is huge, and there are so many goblins."

Baby's mind raced, piecing together a plan. "We need to disable the cauldron. If we can destroy it or disrupt its magic, they won't be able to freeze the town."

Max tilted his head. "But how do we get close enough? They're guarding it like hawks."

Baby glanced at the silver box, its warm energy pulsing faintly in the moonlight. "This might be the answer," she said, her voice thoughtful. "If it's enchanted, it could counteract the magic of the cauldron. But first, we need to create a diversion to draw the goblins away from the house."

Max's tail wagged. "I can howl and lead them on a chase. Goblins hate loud noises, and they'll follow me just to try to shut me up."

Pip nodded. "While they're distracted, I can scout the area and keep watch. Baby, you can focus on the cauldron."

Baby's crimson eyes gleamed with determination. "It's risky, but it's our best shot. Max, be careful. Don't let them catch you."

Max grinned, baring his sharp puppy teeth. "They'll never catch me—I'm too fast."

The trio waited until the goblins' chatter died down, signaling that they had returned to their tasks inside the gingerbread house. Then, under the cover of darkness, they moved into position. Max crouched near the edge of the clearing, his muscles coiled like springs. Pip took to the air, his keen eyes scanning for any stragglers.

Baby hid in the shadows, the silver box tucked securely under her scarf. Her heart raced, but she pushed the fear aside, focusing on the task ahead.

"Go," she whispered.

Max let out a long, mournful howl that echoed through the forest, sending the goblins into a frenzy. They screeched and hissed, abandoning their tasks as they poured out of the gingerbread house in pursuit of the noise. Max darted into the trees, his gray fur blending with the shadows as he led the goblins on a wild chase.

With the coast clear, Baby slipped inside the gingerbread house. The interior was just as she remembered—sticky, sweet, and unnaturally cold. The cauldron bubbled at the center of the room, its icy liquid glowing with an eerie blue light. The decorations and gifts piled around it seemed to pulse with a faint energy, as if the cauldron was feeding on them.

Baby approached cautiously, her vampire senses on high alert. She placed the silver box on the ground beside the cauldron, its warmth spreading through the frosty air. The box seemed to react to the cauldron's magic, glowing brighter as Baby opened it.

Inside was a small, golden star, its surface shimmering with a light that felt alive. Baby's breath caught in her throat. The star radiated warmth, its energy pure and powerful—everything the frost goblins despised.

"This is it," Baby whispered. "This can stop them."

Carefully, she lifted the star and held it over the cauldron. The icy liquid hissed and bubbled violently as the star's warmth began to counteract its magic. The air around the cauldron grew warmer, and the frost on the walls started to melt.

But the noise had alerted the goblins. Baby heard their angry cries as they rushed back toward the house, realizing they had been tricked.

"Pip!" Baby called. "I need that distraction now!"

Pip swooped into the house, knocking over a stack of candy canes and sending them clattering to the ground. The goblins hissed in frustration, their attention divided as they scrambled to stop the chaos.

Baby seized the moment, plunging the golden star into the cauldron. A brilliant burst of light filled the room, blinding the goblins and sending a wave of warmth through the gingerbread house. The cauldron cracked and shattered, its icy magic dissolving into nothingness.

The goblins screamed in defeat, their frosty forms losing their shimmer as the enchanted house began to collapse. Baby darted out just as the structure crumbled behind her, the stolen decorations and gifts spilling into the snow.

Max and Pip joined her, their faces filled with relief and triumph.

"You did it!" Max barked, his tail wagging furiously.

Baby nodded, her crimson eyes shining. "Christmas is safe—for now. But we still have work to do."

With the frost goblins defeated and their plan foiled, the trio began gathering the stolen decorations and gifts, determined to return them to Moonlit Hollow. The town's Christmas spirit had been tested, but thanks to Baby's courage and cleverness, it had emerged stronger than ever.

## Chapter 7: A Holly Jolly Team

The morning sun rose over the Whispering Woods, casting long beams of golden light across the snow-covered landscape. Baby, Pip, and Max had returned to the edge of the forest with their prize: the shattered remains of the frost goblins' cauldron and the silver box containing the golden star. The immediate danger was gone, but the goblins' stolen decorations and gifts were still scattered deep within the forest, hidden among their icy hauls.

"We need reinforcements," Baby announced as she surveyed the forest from a small hill. "The goblins will regroup, and we can't carry everything out of their lair alone."

Pip, perched on her shoulder, tilted his head. "Who can we call? Most of the town doesn't even know what's going on."

Max wagged his tail. "I know someone! Thorn the hedgehog! He's prickly but sneaky, and he loves a good adventure."

Baby smiled. "Thorn's a good choice. We'll also need someone who can scout the area and watch our backs while we work. Do you think we could get Hoots, the magical owl, to help us?"

Pip's wings fluttered with excitement. "Hoots? He's the best! If anyone can spot trouble from the skies, it's him."

"Perfect," Baby said, her crimson eyes gleaming. "Let's split up and gather the team. Pip, you find Hoots. Max, bring Thorn to the clearing near the gingerbread house. I'll prepare a plan while you're gone."

The trio dispersed, moving swiftly through the snowy forest. Baby remained in the clearing, pacing as she thought through their strategy. The goblins would be on high alert, and she needed a way to outsmart them, recover the stolen decorations, and ensure they couldn't rebuild their icy magic.

By the time the sun reached its peak, her friends had returned. Max bounded into the clearing with Thorn trotting behind him. Thorn, a small but formidable hedgehog, wore a tiny green scarf wrapped snugly around his spiky body. His sharp black eyes sparkled with excitement.

"This had better be good," Thorn said, his voice gruff but not unkind. "Max told me it's about saving Christmas. I'm in, but I don't work for free—there'd better be cookies involved."

Baby chuckled. "If we succeed, I'll make sure you get all the cookies you can eat."

Thorn smirked. "Deal."

Moments later, Pip swooped down from the sky, followed by Hoots the magical owl. Hoots was an elegant creature with shimmering silver feathers that sparkled faintly in the sunlight. His deep, knowing eyes surveyed the group as he landed gracefully on a low branch.

"Baby," Hoots said in his smooth, resonant voice, "I've heard whispers of trouble in the forest. Tell me what you need."

Baby explained the situation, outlining the frost goblins' plan and the urgency of recovering the stolen decorations. As she spoke, the team listened intently, their expressions growing more determined.

"Our mission is twofold," Baby concluded. "We need to retrieve the decorations and destroy anything the goblins might use to rebuild their icy magic. Thorn, your job is to sneak into the lair and disable any traps or alarms the goblins have set up. Hoots, you'll keep watch from above and warn us if more goblins are approaching."

Max's tail wagged eagerly. "What about me?"

"You and Pip will create a distraction," Baby said. "We need the goblins focused on you while Thorn and I work. Once the lair is clear, we'll gather everything and get out before they can regroup."

Thorn rolled his eyes. "Typical. The hedgehog gets the dangerous job."

"You're the best at it," Baby replied with a grin. "And besides, I trust you."

Thorn grumbled, but the compliment softened his prickly demeanor. "Fine. Let's do this."

As the team approached the gingerbread house, Baby's heart raced with anticipation. The structure had partially collapsed after the cauldron's destruction, but the goblins had already begun repairing it. The air was thick with their icy magic, and their chatter filled the clearing as they scurried about.

Max and Pip moved into position near the edge of the clearing. Thorn slipped into the shadows, his small, spiky form blending seamlessly with the underbrush. Hoots soared high above, his keen eyes scanning the area for any sign of trouble.

"Ready?" Baby whispered to Max.

Max grinned. "Let's give them a show."

With a loud, enthusiastic howl, Max burst into the clearing, his scruffy fur flying as he darted around the goblins. Pip joined in, divebombing the creatures and knocking over piles of candy canes and ornaments. The goblins shrieked in frustration, abandoning their work to chase the pair.

Baby watched from the shadows as the goblins scattered, leaving their lair unguarded. "Thorn, now!" she whispered.

Thorn moved quickly, his small body slipping through cracks and crevices as he worked to disable the goblins' traps. With his sharp claws and cunning mind, he dismantled tripwires and magical runes, ensuring the path was safe for Baby.

"All clear!" Thorn called softly.

Baby darted into the lair, her vampire speed allowing her to move silently and efficiently. She began gathering the stolen decorations, her paws deftly untangling strands of lights and stacking ornaments into a large burlap sack she had brought along. As she worked, she noticed a second cauldron, smaller than the first but still glowing with a faint, icy light.

"Hoots," she called softly, "keep an eye on that cauldron."

From his perch above, Hoots nodded. "It's weaker than the first, but still dangerous. Be quick."

Baby worked faster, her small frame darting between piles of stolen items. The sack grew heavier with each addition, but she didn't stop. Outside, Max and Pip continued their distraction, leading the goblins further away from the lair.

Finally, the sack was full, and Baby turned to the cauldron. She pulled the golden star from her scarf, its warmth spreading through the icy chamber. With a swift motion, she pressed the star against the cauldron. The icy magic hissed and crackled as the cauldron's surface began to melt, its power dissolving into nothingness.

"It's done," Baby said, her voice steady. "Let's move."

Thorn emerged from the shadows, his expression triumphant. "Nice work, Baby. Now let's get out of here before they realize what we've done."

Baby, Thorn, and Hoots slipped out of the lair just as Max and Pip returned, their distraction complete. The team regrouped in the forest, their mission a success.

"You all did amazing," Baby said, her crimson eyes shining with gratitude. "Thanks to you, Christmas is safe."

Hoots fluffed his feathers proudly. "It was an honor to assist."

Thorn smirked. "Don't forget my cookies."

Max wagged his tail. "That was so much fun! Let's do it again!"

Baby laughed softly. "Maybe next year, Max. For now, let's get these decorations back to Moonlit Hollow."

With their prize in tow, the Holly Jolly Team began their journey home, their hearts full of triumph and the magic of Christmas glowing brightly in their spirits.

## Chapter 8: The Candy Cane Trap

The Holly Jolly Team had made great progress in recovering the stolen decorations, but Baby knew they couldn't rest yet. The frost goblins were clever and determined, and as long as their numbers remained strong, Moonlit Hollow would still be in danger. Baby sat with her friends around a small, magical fire created by Hoots. Its warmth was faint but enough to ward off the biting cold of the Whispering Woods.

"We need to keep the goblins distracted," Baby said, her voice thoughtful. "If we can pull them away from the forest completely, it'll buy us enough time to get the last of the decorations and destroy their remaining magical tools."

Max tilted his head, his amber eyes gleaming with excitement. "What kind of distraction are we talking about? Something big?"

"Something irresistible," Baby replied. "Goblins are drawn to shiny objects and sweets. We'll set a trap using both."

Pip flapped his wings, his face lighting up. "Candy canes and glowing ornaments! They won't be able to resist."

Thorn smirked, his small, spiky body shifting as he rolled a candy cane between his paws. "Sounds like my kind of plan. But how do we make sure they don't figure it out too soon?"

"That's where Hoots comes in," Baby said, turning to the magical owl. "You can watch from above and warn us if they start catching on."

Hoots nodded solemnly, his silver feathers glimmering in the firelight. "I'll keep a close eye on them. What's the plan for when they take the bait?"

"We'll lead them to the clearing near the river," Baby explained. "The ice there is thick enough to hold them, but it's far from their lair. It'll give us enough time to finish what we started."

Max's tail wagged furiously. "I'll help lead them there! I'm great at running in circles."

Baby grinned. "Perfect. Let's get to work."

The team worked through the night, gathering supplies from the stolen stash and the surrounding forest. They strung together strands of glowing ornaments, each one twinkling with an enchanted light that pulsed softly in the darkness. Max and Thorn placed candy canes at strategic points, their red-and-white stripes gleaming enticingly against the snow.

By dawn, the trap was ready. The bait was set in a winding trail that led from the gingerbread house to the river clearing. The ornaments glowed like tiny beacons, and the candy canes sparkled with a sugary glaze that caught the first rays of sunlight.

"Now we wait," Baby said, crouching behind a snowbank with the others. "When they come out, Max, you and Pip will lead them toward the clearing. Thorn, you'll help make sure the path is clear. Hoots, signal us if anything goes wrong."

The forest was eerily silent as they waited, the tension thick in the cold morning air. Then, just as Baby had predicted, the goblins emerged from their lair. Their icy chatter filled the clearing as they noticed the trail of ornaments and candy canes.

One of the goblins, smaller than the others but with sharper claws, scurried forward and sniffed at a candy cane. It let out an excited screech, waving for the others to follow. Within moments, the entire group was scrambling after the trail, their greedy hands snatching at the glowing ornaments and sugary treats.

"It's working," Pip whispered, his wings fluttering with excitement.

"Now's our chance," Baby said. "Max, Pip, go!"

Max let out an excited bark and darted into the open, his scruffy fur flying as he ran ahead of the goblins. Pip swooped down, knocking over a pile of snow to keep the goblins' attention on the trail. The goblins screeched and hissed, chasing after them with surprising speed.

Baby, Thorn, and Hoots stayed behind, ensuring the path was clear before moving toward the goblins' now-abandoned lair. Everything was going according to plan—until the unexpected happened.

A loud, chilling howl echoed through the forest, stopping Baby and the others in their tracks. From the shadows emerged a creature much larger than the frost goblins. Its fur was white as snow, and its glowing blue eyes pierced the darkness. It was the frost goblins' guardian—a creature Baby had only heard about in whispered legends.

"The Frostbeast," Hoots murmured, his voice low and grave. "They must have summoned it to protect their lair."

The Frostbeast let out another bone-chilling howl, its sharp claws glinting as it stomped toward Baby and her team. The goblins, hearing the sound, stopped their chase and began to turn back toward the lair.

"Change of plans!" Baby shouted. "Thorn, stay with me. Hoots, warn Max and Pip!"

Hoots took to the skies, his powerful wings cutting through the air as he raced toward Max and Pip. Meanwhile, Baby and Thorn stood their ground, facing the Frostbeast. Thorn's spikes bristled, and Baby crouched low, her crimson eyes locked on the massive creature.

The Frostbeast lunged, its claws swiping through the air with terrifying speed. Baby dodged to the side, her vampire reflexes allowing her to evade the attack. Thorn rolled into a spiky ball and launched himself at the creature's leg, his sharp quills piercing its icy hide.

The Frostbeast roared in pain, but its focus remained on Baby. She darted around it, leading it away from the lair while Thorn continued to harry its movements.

"Keep it busy!" Baby called to Thorn. "We just need to buy time!"

Thorn grunted in response, his sharp quills gleaming as he rolled toward the creature again. Despite its size and strength, the Frostbeast struggled to keep up with their speed and agility.

Meanwhile, Max and Pip returned, having successfully led the goblins far enough away. Hoots landed beside them, his feathers ruffled but his voice calm. "The Frostbeast is guarding the lair. Baby and Thorn are holding it off, but we need to act quickly."

Max growled, his amber eyes blazing with determination. "Let's finish this."

The team regrouped, their combined efforts overwhelming the Frostbeast. Using the golden star's warmth, Baby delivered the final blow, melting the icy creature into a harmless puddle of water. With the Frostbeast defeated and the goblins distracted, the team raided the lair and recovered the remaining decorations and magical tools.

By the time the sun set, Moonlit Hollow's Christmas spirit was safe, thanks to Baby's cleverness and her holly jolly team. The candy cane trap had worked, and despite the unexpected twist, they had emerged victorious. But Baby knew their journey wasn't over yet—there were still lessons to learn and a town to protect.

## Chapter 9: A Snowstorm Surprise

The journey back to Moonlit Hollow began under clear skies, the silver moon casting a serene glow over the snow-covered forest. Baby, Pip, Max, Thorn, and Hoots moved swiftly, the burlap sack of stolen decorations and gifts dragging behind them on a makeshift sled. The team's spirits were high after defeating the frost goblins and their Frost-beast guardian, but Baby couldn't shake the feeling that their victory had come too easily.

As they reached the halfway point between the Whispering Woods and the outskirts of Moonlit Hollow, the wind began to pick up. At first, it was a soft, chilling breeze, but within minutes it turned into a fierce, howling gale. Snowflakes swirled around them in an ever-thickening flurry, and the forest grew darker as heavy clouds rolled in to blot out the moonlight.

"Baby, this storm doesn't feel natural," Hoots said, his deep voice carrying a note of unease as he perched on a low branch, his silver feathers ruffled against the wind.

"It's not," Baby replied, her crimson eyes narrowing as she surveyed their surroundings. "The frost goblins must have cast a spell before we destroyed their lair. They're trying to stop us from reaching Moonlit Hollow."

Max's ears flattened against his head as he pushed through the snow, his amber eyes wide. "What do we do, Baby? I can barely see two feet in front of me!"

Pip fluttered to Baby's shoulder, his wings struggling against the wind. "If we can't find our way back, all our work will have been for nothing. The decorations, the gifts—it'll all be lost!"

Baby's mind raced. The blizzard was growing stronger by the second, and the sled was becoming harder to pull through the deepening snow.

She knew they needed to act quickly before the storm completely overwhelmed them.

"Everyone stay close to me," she said, her voice steady but firm. "I'll light the way."

Pip tilted his head. "Light the way? How?"

Baby reached up and tapped the glowing collar around her neck—a gift from Santa Claus himself, enchanted with a warm, golden light that shone brightest in times of need. As she activated it, the collar emitted a brilliant, steady glow that pierced through the swirling snow. The golden light illuminated the path ahead, creating a beacon for her friends to follow.

"Whoa," Max breathed, his tail wagging despite the storm. "That's amazing, Baby!"

"Let's move," Baby said, taking the lead. "Stay close, and don't lose sight of the light."

The storm raged around them as they pressed forward, the glowing collar guiding them through the blinding snow. The wind howled like a living thing, and the snow stung their faces as they trudged through the drifts. Thorn grumbled as he rolled himself into a spiky ball to shield against the worst of the wind, while Hoots flew low, his sharp eyes scanning for any dangers hidden in the storm.

"Are we even going the right way?" Pip shouted over the howling wind, his voice tinged with doubt.

"We are," Baby replied, her tone unwavering. "Just trust me."

The forest seemed endless in the blizzard, the familiar landmarks obscured by the snow. Baby's glowing collar was the only thing keeping them on track, its warm light a comforting contrast to the freezing cold.

As they pushed forward, a sudden, eerie sound cut through the storm—a low, mournful wail that sent shivers down their spines. The group froze, their eyes darting around in search of the source.

"What was that?" Max whispered, his fur bristling.

Hoots landed beside Baby, his feathers puffed up against the cold. "It's the wind... or so it seems."

Baby's crimson eyes narrowed. "No, it's not just the wind. Something's out there."

The wail grew louder, and through the swirling snow, a faint figure emerged. It was tall and thin, with long, flowing robes made of frost and ice. Its face was obscured by a hood, but its glowing blue eyes burned like frozen fire. The air around it grew colder as it approached, and the snow seemed to move with it, swirling in unnatural patterns.

"The Frost Wraith," Hoots said, his voice barely above a whisper. "A spirit of the storm, summoned by the goblins to stop us."

Baby stepped forward, her glowing collar casting light on the wraith. "We don't want to fight you," she said, her voice calm but firm. "Let us pass, and no harm will come to you."

The Frost Wraith didn't respond. Instead, it raised an icy hand, and the wind howled louder as a wall of snow rose between the group and the path ahead.

"We don't have time for this!" Pip shouted, his small claws clutching Baby's fur. "What do we do?"

Baby's mind worked quickly. She knew the wraith was powerful, but it wasn't invincible. The golden light from her collar was their best chance against the spirit's icy magic.

"Stay behind me," she commanded. "I'll handle this."

Baby stepped forward, her glowing collar shining brighter with every step. The Frost Wraith hissed and recoiled as the golden light pierced through its icy form. It raised its hands to summon another wave of snow, but Baby stood her ground, her eyes blazing with determination.

"This storm ends now," she said, her voice echoing with authority.

With a burst of energy, the light from Baby's collar intensified, filling the clearing with a warm, golden glow. The Frost Wraith let out a final, mournful wail before dissolving into a flurry of snowflakes, its icy magic dispelled by the light.

The storm began to subside, the howling wind fading to a gentle breeze. The snow stopped falling, and the clouds parted to reveal the moon once more. Baby turned to her friends, her glowing collar dimming as the danger passed.

"It's over," she said, her voice soft but triumphant. "Let's get these decorations back to Moonlit Hollow."

As the team continued their journey, the forest grew brighter and more familiar. The lights of Moonlit Hollow appeared on the horizon, a beacon of hope and warmth after their harrowing journey. The townsfolk greeted them with cheers and gratitude as they returned the stolen decorations and gifts, their hearts filled with the spirit of Christmas.

That night, as Baby and her friends rested by the fire in her cozy cottage, she reflected on their adventure. They had faced storms, goblins, and even a Frost Wraith, but their determination and teamwork had prevailed.

Christmas was saved, and Moonlit Hollow was once again a place of light, warmth, and magic—all thanks to a brave vampire terrier and her holly jolly team.

## Chapter 10: Saving the Town Tree

The air in Moonlit Hollow was filled with the sounds of Christmas cheer as the townsfolk celebrated the return of their stolen decorations and gifts. The town square glimmered with renewed life, strings of lights twinkling like stars and ornaments sparkling on every tree and lamppost. At the center of it all stood the town's Christmas tree—a towering evergreen adorned with glowing bulbs, shimmering tinsel, and a golden star at its peak. It was the pride of Moonlit Hollow, a symbol of togetherness and joy.

Baby and her friends stood near the tree, watching as the townsfolk sang carols and laughed with one another. For a moment, everything felt perfect. But Baby's sharp senses told her otherwise.

Something wasn't right.

Her crimson eyes scanned the square, catching faint flickers of movement in the shadows beyond the festive lights. The air grew colder, a tell-tale sign of lingering frost goblin magic. Baby's ears perked up, catching a faint, high-pitched chatter that was unmistakable.

"They're here," she said, her voice low but urgent.

Pip, perched on her shoulder, fluttered his wings nervously. "The goblins? Here? But we destroyed their lair!"

"They must have regrouped," Hoots said, his deep voice calm but serious. "And it looks like they've set their sights on the town tree."

Max growled softly, his amber eyes fixed on the shadows. "They're not taking it. Not after everything we've done to save Christmas."

Baby nodded. "We won't let them. But we need a plan."

The team huddled together, their breath visible in the crisp night air as they whispered their strategy. The frost goblins were clever and quick, but Baby and her friends had something they didn't—unity and the true spirit of the season.

As the townsfolk continued their celebrations, the frost goblins began to creep closer to the tree. Their small, wiry bodies blended with the snow, and their glowing blue eyes scanned the square for any sign of danger. One of the goblins, slightly larger than the others and wearing a crown of icicles, barked out commands in their strange, tinkling language. It was clear this goblin was their leader.

The goblins moved silently, their icy claws reaching for the tree's lower branches. But just as they prepared to strike, a loud, cheerful bark echoed through the square.

"Not so fast!" Max shouted, bounding into the open.

The goblins hissed in surprise, their icy bodies shimmering as they turned toward the werewolf puppy. Max darted around the tree, wagging his tail and barking loudly to draw their attention.

"Hey, over here!" Pip called, swooping down to knock over a stack of candy canes near the tree. The clattering noise sent the goblins into a frenzy, their icy magic crackling as they scrambled to chase the distractions.

From her hiding spot beneath the tree, Baby watched the chaos unfold. She had positioned herself at the base of the trunk, her glowing collar dimmed to avoid detection. Thorn was nearby, his small, spiky form camouflaged in the tinsel as he prepared to defend the tree from any goblins that got too close.

Hoots circled above, his sharp eyes scanning the square for any sign of reinforcements. "The leader is near the tree," he called softly to Baby. "If we can stop them, the others will retreat."

Baby's eyes locked onto the goblin leader, who was now barking out orders to its minions. Unlike the others, this goblin carried a staff made of ice, its tip glowing with a faint blue light. It was clear the staff was the source of their remaining magic.

"Leave the leader to me," Baby said, her voice steady. "Thorn, stay ready in case they get past me."

Thorn grunted in agreement, his sharp quills bristling. "Just say the word."

Baby crept forward, her small frame silent against the snow. The goblin leader was focused on the tree, its icy claws reaching for the golden star at the top. Baby's crimson eyes narrowed as she prepared to strike.

With a burst of vampire speed, she leapt into the air, landing gracefully on a low branch. The goblin leader screeched in surprise, its staff raised defensively as Baby lunged toward it. Her glowing collar flared to life, casting a warm, golden light that sent the goblin reeling.

"You're not taking this tree," Baby growled, her voice firm but calm. "Christmas isn't something you can steal."

The goblin leader hissed, swinging its staff in a wide arc. Baby dodged effortlessly, her quick reflexes allowing her to stay one step ahead. She circled the goblin, her collar's light growing brighter with each step.

"Why do you hate Christmas so much?" she asked, her voice softer now. "What are you trying to prove?"

The goblin paused, its icy eyes flickering with something that almost resembled sadness. For a brief moment, Baby saw past its frost-covered exterior to the small, vulnerable creature underneath. It wasn't evil—it was lonely.

"You don't have to ruin Christmas to feel powerful," Baby said gently. "There's enough magic for everyone, including you."

The goblin leader hesitated, its staff trembling in its hands. Behind it, the other goblins stopped their chaos, their icy forms melting slightly as they watched the scene unfold.

Taking a chance, Baby stepped closer. "Join us," she said, her voice warm and inviting. "Christmas is about togetherness, not just lights and gifts. You don't have to be alone."

The goblin leader lowered its staff, its icy glow fading as the warmth of Baby's collar filled the square. The other goblins followed suit, their claws retracting as they gathered around the tree. The townsfolk watched in awe, their fear replaced by curiosity and wonder.

Max, Pip, Thorn, and Hoots joined Baby, their faces filled with pride as the goblins began to help decorate the tree instead of destroying it. The leader placed its staff at the base of the trunk, the ice melting into a sparkling pool that reflected the golden lights above.

By the time the star at the top of the tree was lit, Moonlit Hollow had become a beacon of light and warmth, a place where even frost goblins could find belonging. Baby and her friends had not only saved the tree—they had shown the true spirit of Christmas: forgiveness, kindness, and love.

As the bells rang out across the town square, Baby looked up at the tree, her heart full of pride and joy. "Merry Christmas," she whispered, her glowing collar shining brighter than ever.

## Chapter 11: A Christmas Truce

The frost goblins stood awkwardly near the town's Christmas tree, their glowing blue eyes flickering with uncertainty. Their leader, the one with the now-melted ice staff, shuffled its clawed feet, glancing nervously at Baby. It was clear they weren't used to being welcomed, let alone invited to a celebration as grand as Moonlit Hollow's Christmas festival.

Baby's glowing collar dimmed slightly as she turned to face the gathered crowd. The townsfolk of Moonlit Hollow were frozen in place, their faces a mixture of curiosity and apprehension. The frost goblins had been their tormentors for weeks, stealing decorations and gifts, and even attempting to freeze the entire town. To see them standing harmlessly beneath the tree, looking almost vulnerable, was a sight no one had expected.

Baby stepped forward, her small frame radiating confidence. "Everyone," she said, her voice calm but commanding, "the frost goblins weren't trying to ruin Christmas—they just didn't know how to be part of it."

A murmur rippled through the crowd. Mrs. Garland, the town baker, stepped forward cautiously. "What do you mean, Baby? They stole from us, caused trouble... Why would they do that if they wanted to be included?"

Baby glanced back at the goblin leader, whose icy eyes met hers for a brief moment. "They've been watching us," she explained. "They saw the joy, the decorations, the togetherness—and they didn't understand it. They felt left out, like there wasn't a place for them in our celebrations. So they tried to take what they couldn't have."

Pip fluttered down to perch on Baby's shoulder. "We all know what it's like to feel left out," he said, his voice soft but firm. "Christmas is about including everyone, right?"

Max wagged his tail, his amber eyes shining with determination. "Yeah! If we can forgive them, we can show them what Christmas is really about."

The goblins shifted uncomfortably, their icy claws fidgeting as they listened. Their leader stepped forward, hesitating before bowing its head slightly toward Baby.

"You... invite us?" it said in a voice that tinkled like wind chimes, the first words it had spoken since their confrontation at the tree.

Baby nodded, her crimson eyes warm and inviting. "Yes. You're welcome here. But no more stealing, no more freezing the town. If you want to be part of Christmas, you have to help make it special."

The goblin leader tilted its head, clearly taken aback by the offer. Slowly, it turned to its followers and barked out a few words in their strange, musical language. The other goblins responded with cautious nods and murmurs, their icy forms softening slightly as they began to warm to the idea.

The transformation was nothing short of miraculous. Under Baby's guidance, the frost goblins began to work alongside the townsfolk to repair the damage they had caused. They helped hang ornaments on the Christmas tree, their nimble claws perfect for reaching the highest branches. They strung lights along the rooftops, their icy magic adding a shimmering, frosted effect that made the decorations even more beautiful.

Thorn, ever practical, took charge of organizing the candy cane display. "You goblins are pretty good with sweets," he admitted gruffly as one goblin skillfully shaped a candy cane into an intricate spiral. "But don't get any ideas—I'm still keeping an eye on you."

Hoots circled above the square, his sharp eyes ensuring everything remained peaceful. "It seems they're genuinely trying," he said to Baby as he landed on a nearby lamppost. "You've done something extraordinary here."

Baby smiled. "It wasn't just me. Everyone here is part of this."

As the frost goblins worked, the townsfolk began to warm up to them. Mrs. Garland offered them steaming mugs of hot cocoa, which they accepted hesitantly at first. The warmth seemed to surprise them, melting the frost on their claws as they sipped the sweet drink. The children of Moonlit Hollow, initially frightened, started to play games with the smaller goblins, chasing each other around the square and laughing.

By evening, the town square was more beautiful than it had ever been. The Christmas tree glowed brightly, its lights reflecting off the fresh layer of snow. The air was filled with the sound of carols, the aroma of freshly baked cookies, and the laughter of both townsfolk and goblins alike.

The goblin leader approached Baby, its glowing eyes now soft and warm. "Thank you," it said in its musical voice, bowing low. "We... never had this before. Always... outside. Watching. Now... part."

Baby placed a gentle paw on the goblin's icy claw. "You're part of it now. Christmas is for everyone who wants to share its magic."

Max trotted over, his tail wagging furiously. "This is the best Christmas ever! We saved the town, made new friends, and the tree looks amazing!"

Pip flitted to Baby's other shoulder, his small face beaming with pride. "And it's all thanks to you, Baby. You showed them what Christmas is really about."

Baby's glowing collar shone brightly as she looked out over the square. The frost goblins were no longer enemies—they were part of the town's celebration, their icy magic adding a unique and beautiful touch to the festivities.

As the golden star atop the tree twinkled against the night sky, Baby felt a deep sense of fulfillment. She had not only protected Moonlit Hollow but had also brought its residents closer together, proving that the true spirit of Christmas could melt even the coldest hearts.

"Merry Christmas, everyone," Baby said softly, her voice carrying through the square.

And for the first time in their frosty lives, the goblins responded in unison, their tinkling voices ringing out like bells:
"Merry Christmas."

## Chapter 12: A Moonlit Christmas

The snow-covered streets of Moonlit Hollow sparkled under the soft glow of the full moon. The frost goblins, now cheerful and brimming with holiday spirit, worked side by side with the townsfolk to restore every stolen decoration and gift. The golden star atop the town's towering Christmas tree shone brightly, its light spreading a warm glow that reached every corner of the square.

Baby stood at the base of the tree, her crimson eyes scanning the bustling activity around her. She couldn't help but feel a swell of pride as she watched the frost goblins, who had once been the source of chaos, eagerly help hang ornaments and string lights. Their icy magic, now playful and harmless, added a shimmering frost effect to the decorations, making the town even more enchanting.

### Restoring the Decorations

The goblin leader, now affectionately nicknamed "Frosty" by the children, approached Baby with a small box of ornaments. "Where... these go?" it asked in its soft, tinkling voice.

Baby smiled, gesturing to a nearby lamppost. "Those are for the posts around the square. Just hang them where the hooks are."

Frosty nodded and shuffled off, its icy claws carefully handling the delicate ornaments. Nearby, Max was enthusiastically directing a group of smaller goblins as they decorated a row of evergreen garlands.

"No, no, that goes on the left side!" Max barked playfully, wagging his tail. "Perfect! Great job, everyone!"

Pip flitted above the scene, carrying a strand of lights in his tiny claws. "Max, don't forget to leave room for the candy canes!" he called, his wings fluttering as he hovered near a group of children who were threading garlands with gumdrops.

Hoots, perched on the highest branch of the Christmas tree, oversaw the entire operation. His wise, calming presence ensured that everything ran smoothly. "A little to the left," he called to a goblin who was adjusting the star atop a smaller tree nearby. "Perfect. The symmetry is key."

Even Thorn, ever the skeptic, had warmed up to the goblins. He stood near the town's nativity display, supervising as a pair of goblins carefully dusted the scene with enchanted snow. "Not bad," Thorn muttered, his prickly demeanor softening. "Just don't drop anything."

**A Town Transformed**

By the time the sun dipped below the horizon, Moonlit Hollow had been transformed into a winter wonderland. Every house was adorned with twinkling lights, every lamppost wrapped in garlands, and every tree glimmered with ornaments and frost. The stolen gifts had been returned to their rightful places, wrapped and waiting under the glowing Christmas tree.

The townsfolk gathered in the square, their faces lit with joy and gratitude. Children ran through the snow, laughing and playing with the goblins, who now seemed more like mischievous but lovable holiday helpers. Mrs. Garland handed out steaming mugs of hot cocoa, while the town's choir began to sing carols that echoed warmly through the crisp night air.

At the center of it all stood Baby, her glowing collar dimly pulsing in time with the twinkling lights around her. She watched as the townsfolk embraced the goblins, offering them cookies, scarves, and even small gifts. For the first time, the frost goblins were part of something bigger than themselves—a community filled with love and warmth.

**The Christmas Eve Celebration**

The evening's highlight came when the entire town gathered beneath the Christmas tree. The choir sang a final carol, their voices rising in harmony as the golden star atop the tree sparkled brighter than ever. Baby stepped forward, joined by her friends and Frosty, to address the crowd.

"This Christmas is special," Baby began, her voice steady but filled with emotion. "Not just because we've saved our decorations and gifts, but because we've shown that the true spirit of the season is about forgiveness, kindness, and bringing everyone together."

The crowd erupted into cheers, and Frosty stepped forward timidly, holding up a small ornament made of ice. It shimmered like crystal, reflecting the lights of the tree. "For... town," Frosty said, its voice soft but clear.

The townsfolk gasped in awe as Baby took the ornament and hung it on the tree. The moment it touched the branch, the entire tree sparkled with a magical frost that danced like starlight, eliciting another round of cheers and applause.

**Baby's Moment of Reflection**

As the celebration continued, Baby found a quiet moment to sit near the edge of the square. Pip landed beside her, his wings folding neatly. "You did it, Baby," he said, his voice filled with pride. "You saved Christmas."

Baby looked up at the glowing tree, her crimson eyes reflecting its light. "We all did," she replied. "Everyone played a part. And I think we've given the goblins something they've never had before—a place where they belong."

Max trotted over, his tail wagging as he nudged Baby's paw. "You're a hero, Baby. A real Christmas hero."

Hoots landed gracefully on a nearby bench, his wise gaze fixed on Baby. "Even vampires," he said with a hint of a smile, "can make Christmas magical."

Baby chuckled softly, her glowing collar casting a warm light on her face. "I never thought I'd be part of something like this," she admitted. "Christmas was always just another day for me. But now... now I see what makes it so special."

**A Moonlit Christmas**

As midnight approached, the moon rose higher in the sky, casting its silvery light over the town. The celebrations began to wind down as families returned home, their hearts full of joy and gratitude. The frost goblins, now officially welcomed into the community, stayed behind to help clean up, their playful chatter filling the square.

Baby stood beneath the tree with her friends, the golden star shining brightly above them. For the first time, she felt truly at home in Moonlit Hollow, surrounded by those she cared about and the magic of the season.

"Merry Christmas, everyone," Baby said softly, her voice carrying on the crisp night air.

"Merry Christmas!" her friends replied in unison, their faces glowing with happiness.

As the town settled into a peaceful, moonlit Christmas Eve, Baby knew one thing for certain: the magic of Christmas wasn't just in the decorations, the gifts, or the tree—it was in the love and togetherness that brought everyone, even frost goblins, together under the same starry sky.

**Epilogue: The Magic of Moonlit Hollow**

The first light of dawn painted the snowy rooftops of Moonlit Hollow in soft shades of gold and pink. The festivities had long since ended, but the warm glow of Christmas magic lingered in every corner of the town. Snowflakes fell gently from the sky, blanketing the cobblestone streets in a fresh layer of white, muffling the world in a serene, peaceful quiet.

Inside Baby's cozy cottage, the crackling fire cast dancing shadows across the walls, its warmth chasing away the lingering chill of the winter night. Baby, the brave vampire terrier, lay curled up in her favorite spot on a plush red blanket near the hearth. Her glowing collar, now dimmed to a soft, steady pulse, reflected the flickering flames, casting a warm golden light around the room.

Pip was perched on the mantle above the fire, his tiny wings folded neatly as he gazed down at the scene below. "You know, Baby," he said softly, his voice filled with contentment, "this has to be the best Christmas we've ever had."

Baby stretched her paws, letting out a soft yawn before smiling up at her winged friend. "It wasn't just the best—it was magical. I didn't think I'd ever be part of something like this."

Max, the scruffy werewolf puppy, lay sprawled out on the rug beside Baby, his tail thumping lazily against the floor. "You were amazing,

Baby. You saved Christmas! And not just for Moonlit Hollow—for everyone."

Thorn, ever the realist, was nestled in a small pile of tinsel near the Christmas tree. "Let's not get carried away," he grumbled, though his prickly demeanor was softened by the satisfied glint in his sharp eyes. "We all played our part."

Hoots, perched on the back of an armchair, ruffled his feathers as he added, "Indeed we did. But Baby showed us something more than bravery. She showed us that even the coldest hearts can be warmed with a little kindness."

The room fell into a comfortable silence as each of them reflected on the events of the past few days. The frost goblins had been welcomed into the town's celebrations, the stolen decorations and gifts had been returned, and Moonlit Hollow had become a beacon of Christmas magic for all who saw it.

Baby's crimson eyes softened as she stared into the flames. "It wasn't just about saving Christmas," she said quietly. "It was about showing everyone, even the goblins, that they belong. That's what Christmas is really about—finding ways to bring people together, no matter how different they might seem."

Pip fluttered down to sit beside her. "And you did that, Baby. You made it happen."

**The Future Beckons**

As the fire crackled and the snow continued to fall outside, Baby's thoughts drifted to the future. The frost goblins had promised to help with next year's decorations, their icy magic now a cherished addition to Moonlit Hollow's traditions. She wondered what other adventures awaited her and her friends—what new challenges they might face and what new friendships they might forge.

"Do you think next Christmas will be this exciting?" Max asked, his voice sleepy but hopeful.

Baby chuckled softly, her tail curling around her paws. "Who knows? But whatever happens, I know we'll face it together."

Thorn snorted from his tinsel nest. "As long as it doesn't involve more candy canes. I'm still picking bits of sugar out of my quills."

The group laughed, the sound light and full of joy. Even Hoots, normally so composed, let out a soft hoot of amusement.

**Dreaming of Christmas Adventures**

As the warmth of the fire lulled them into a drowsy contentment, Baby let her eyes close, her mind filled with dreams of more Christmas adventures. She imagined snowy forests filled with hidden treasures, enchanted stars that needed rescuing, and magical creatures waiting to befriend them. But most of all, she imagined Moonlit Hollow glowing brighter with each passing year, its spirit of love and togetherness growing stronger.

Outside, the snow continued to fall, blanketing the town in a hushed stillness. The Christmas tree in the square twinkled softly, its golden star a beacon of hope and magic against the wintry sky. The frost goblins, now at home in Moonlit Hollow, worked quietly to add a final touch of frost to the rooftops, their laughter carrying faintly on the cold breeze.

In her cozy cottage, surrounded by her friends, Baby slept soundly, her glowing collar casting a gentle light over the room. The magic of Christmas had touched every heart in Moonlit Hollow, and Baby knew deep down that this was only the beginning.

For even in the quiet of the snowy morning, as the town rested from its celebrations, the promise of new adventures—and more magical Christmases—lingered in the air. And Baby, the brave vampire terrier, was ready for whatever came next.

"Merry Christmas," she murmured softly in her sleep, her voice carrying the warmth of the season.

And outside, beneath the moonlit sky, it seemed as though the entire town whispered back:

"Merry Christmas, Baby."

## Message from the Author:

I hope you enjoyed this book, I love astrology and knew there was not a book such as this out on the shelf. I love metaphysical items as well. Please check out my other books:

-Life of Government Benefits

-My life of Hell

-My life with Hydrocephalus

-Red Sky

-World Domination:Woman's rule

-World Domination:Woman's Rule 2: The War

-Life and Banishment of Apophis: book 1

-The Kidney Friendly Diet

-The Ultimate Hemp Cookbook

-Creating a Dispensary(legally)

-Cleanliness throughout life: the importance of showering from childhood to adulthood.

-Strong Roots: The Risks of Overcoddling children

-Hemp Horoscopes: Cosmic Insights and Earthly Healing

- Celestial Hemp Navigating the Zodiac: Through the Green Cosmos

-Astrological Hemp: Aligning The Stars with Earth's Ancient Herb

-The Astrological Guide to Hemp: Stars, Signs, and Sacred Leaves

-Green Growth: Innovative Marketing Strategies for your Hemp Products and Dispensary

-Cosmic Cannabis

-Astrological Munchies

-Henry The Hemp

-Zodiacal Roots: The Astrological Soul Of Hemp

**- Green Constellations: Intersection of Hemp and Zodiac**

-Hemp in The Houses: An astrological Adventure Through The Cannabis Galaxy

-Galactic Ganja Guide

Heavenly Hemp

Zodiac Leaves

Doctor Who Astrology

Cannastrology

Stellar Satvias and Cosmic Indicas

<u>Celestial Cannabis: A Zodiac Journey</u>

AstroHerbology: The Sky and The Soil: Volume 1

AstroHerbology:Celestial Cannabis:Volume 2

Cosmic Cannabis Cultivation

The Starry Guide to Herbal Harmony: Volume 1

The Starry Guide to Herbal Harmony: Cannabis Universe: Volume 2

Yugioh Astrology: Astrological Guide to Deck, Duels and more

Nightmare Mansion: Echoes of The Abyss

**Nightmare Mansion 2: Legacy of Shadows**

**Nightmare Mansion 3: Shadows of the Forgotten**

Nightmare Mansion 4: Echoes of the Damned

The Life and Banishment of Apophis: Book 2

Nightmare Mansion: Halls of Despair

<u>Healing with Herb: Cannabis and Hydrocephalus</u>

**<u>Planetary Pot: Aligning with Astrological Herbs: Volume 1</u>**

**Fast Track to Freedom: 30 Days to Financial Independence Using AI, Assets, and Agile Hustles**

**<u>Cosmic Hemp Pathways</u>**

**How to Become Financially Free in 30 Days: 10,000 Paths to Prosperity**

**Zodiacal Herbage: Astrological Insights: Volume 1**

Nightmare Mansion: Whispers in the Walls

The Daleks Invade Atlantis

**Henry the hemp and Hydrocephalus**

10X The Kidney Friendly Diet
Cannabis Universe: Adult coloring book
**Hemp Astrology: The Healing Power of the Stars**
**Zodiacal Herbage: Astrological Insights: Cannabis Universe: Volume 2**
**<u>Planetary Pot: Aligning with Astrological Herbs: Cannabis Universes: Volume 2</u>**
Doctor Who Meets the Replicators and SG-1: The Ultimate Battle for Survival
Nightmare Mansion: Curse of the Blood Moon
**<u>The Celestial Stoner: A Guide to the Zodiac</u>**
**Cosmic Pleasures: Sex Toy Astrology for Every Sign**
Hydrocephalus Astrology: Navigating the Stars and Healing Waters
**Lapis and the Mischievous Chocolate Bar**

Celestial Positions: Sexual Astrology for Every Sign
Apophis's Shadow Work Journal: : A Journey of Self-Discovery and Healing
**Kinky Cosmos: Sexual Kink Astrology for Every Sign**
**Digital Cosmos: The Astrological Digimon Compendium**
**Stellar Seeds: The Cosmic Guide to Growing with Astrology**
Apophis's Daily Gratitude Journal

Cat Astrology: Feline Mysteries of the Cosmos
**The Cosmic Kama Sutra: An Astrological Guide to Sexual Positions**
**Unleash Your Potential: A Guided Journal Powered by AI Insights**
**Whispers of the Enchanted Grove**

Cosmic Pleasures: An Astrological Guide to Sexual Kinks

369, 12 Manifestation Journal

Whisper of the nocturne journal(blank journal for writing or drawing)

The Boogey Book

Locked In Reflection: A Chastity Journey Through Locktober

Generating Wealth Quickly:

How to Generate $100,000 in 24 Hours

Star Magic: Harness the Power of the Universe

The Flatulence Chronicles: A Fart Journal for Self-Discovery

The Doctor and The Death Moth

Seize the Day: A Personal Seizure Tracking Journal

The Ultimate Boogeyman Safari: A Journey into the Boogie World and Beyond

**Whispers of Samhain: 1,000 Spells of Love, Luck, and Lunar Magic: Samhain Spell Book**

**Apophis's guides:**

**Witch's Spellbook Crafting Guide for Halloween**

**<u>Frost & Flame: The Enchanted Yule Grimoire of 1000 Winter Spells</u>**

**<u>The Ultimate Boogey Goo Guide & Spooky Activities for Halloween Fun</u>**

Harmony of the Scales: A Libra's Spellcraft for Balance and Beauty

The Enchanted Advent: 36 Days of Christmas Wonders


**Nightmare Mansion: The Labyrinth of Screams**

Harvest of Enchantment: 1,000 Spells of Gratitude, Love, and Fortune for Thanksgiving

The Boogey Chronicles: A Journal of Nightly Encounters and Shadowy Secrets

The 12 Days of Financial Freedom: A Step-by-Step Christmas Countdown to Transform Your Finances

Sigil of the Eternal Spiral Blank Journal

A Christmas Feast: Timeless Recipes for Every Meal

Holiday Stress-Free Solutions: A Survival Guide to Thriving During the Festive Season

Yu-Gi-Oh! Holiday Gifting Mastery: The Ultimate Guide for Fans and Newcomers Alike

Holiday Harmony: A Hydrocephalus Survival Guide for the Festive Season

Celestial Craft: The Witch's Almanac for 2025 – A Cosmic Guide to Manifestations, Moons, and Mystical Events

Doctor Who: The Toymaker's Winter Wonderland

Tulsa King Unveiled: A Thrilling Guide to Stallone's Mafia Masterpiece

Pendulum Craft: A Complete Guide to Crafting and Using Personalized Divination Tools

Nightmare Mansion: Santa's Eternal Eve

Starlight Noel: A Cosmic Journey through Christmas Mysteries

The Dark Architect: Unlocking the Blueprint of Existence

Surviving the Embrace: The Ultimate Guide to Encounters with The Hugging Molly

The Enchanted Codex: Secrets of the Craft for Witches, Wiccans, and Pagans

Harvest of Gratitude: A Complete Thanksgiving Guide

Yuletide Essentials: A Complete Guide to an Authentic and Magical Christmas

Celestial Smokes: A Cosmic Guide to Cigars and Astrology

Living in Balance: A Comprehensive Survival Guide to Thriving with Diabetes Insipidus

Cosmic Symbiosis: The Venom Zodiac Chronicles

***The Cursed Paw of Ambition***

Cosmic Symbiosis: The Astrological Venom Journal

Celestial Wonders Unfold: A Stargazer's Guide to the Cosmos (2024-2029)

The Ultimate Black Friday Prepper's Guide: Mastering Shopping Strategies and Savings

*Cosmic Sales: The Astrological Guide to Black Friday Shopping*

Legends of the Corn Mother and Other Harvest Myths

Whispers of the Harvest: The Corn Mother's Journal

The Evergreen Spellbook

The Doctor Meets the Boogeyman

The White Witch of Rose Hall's SpellBook

**The Gingerbread Golem's Shadow: A Study in Sweet Darkness**

**The Gingerbread Golem Codex: An Academic Exploration of Sweet Myths**

The Gingerbread Golem Grimoire: Sweet Magicks and Spells for the Festive Witch

**The Curse of the Gingerbread Golem**

10-minute Christmas Crafts for kids

**<u>Christmas Crisis Solutions: The Ultimate Last-Minute Survival Guide</u>**

Gingerbread Golem Recipes: Holiday Treats with a Magical Twist

***The Infinite Key: Unlocking Mystical Secrets of the Ages***

Enchanted Yule: A Wiccan and Pagan Guide to a Magical and Memorable Season

Dinosaurs of Power: Unlocking Ancient Magick

Astro-Dinos: The Cosmic Guide to Prehistoric Wisdom

Gallifrey's Yule Logs: A Festive Doctor Who Cookbook

**The Dino Grimoire: Secrets of Prehistoric Magick**

**The Gift They Never Knew They Needed**

*The Gingerbread Golem's Culinary Alchemy: Enchanting Recipes for a Sweetly Dark Feast*

A Time Lord Christmas: Holiday Adventures with the Doctor

**Krampusproofing Your Home: Defensive Strategies for Yule**

Silent Frights: A Collection of Christmas Creepypastas to Chill Your Bones

***Santa Raptor's Jolly Carnage: A Dino-Claus Christmas Tale***

Prehistoric Palettes: A Dino Wicca Coloring Journey
The Christmas Wishkeeper Chronicles
The Starlight Sleigh: A Holiday Journey
*Elf Secrets: The True Magic of the North Pole*
Candy Cane Conjurations
***Cooking with Kids: Recipes Under 20 Minutes***
Doctor Who: The TARDIS Confiscation
*The Anxiety First Aid Kit: Quick Tools to Calm Your Mind*
Frosty Whispers: A Winter's Tale
The Infinite Key: Unlocking the Secrets to Prosperity, Resilience, and Purpose
The Grasping Void: Why You'll Regret This Purchase
Astrology for Busy Bees: Star Signs Simplified
***The Instant Focus Formula: Cut Through the Noise***
The Secret Language of Colors: Unlocking the Emotional Codes
Sacred Fossil Chronicles: Blank Journal
**The Christmas Cottage Miracle**
**Feeding Frenzy: Graboid-Inspired Recipes**
**Manifest in Minutes: The Quick Law of Attraction Guide**
**The Symbiote Chronicles: Doctor Who's Venomous Journey**
**Think Tiny, Grow Big: The Minimalist Mindset**
**The Energy Key: Unlocking Limitless Motivation**
New Year, New Magic: Manifesting Your Best Year Yet
Unstoppable You: Mastering Confidence in Minutes
Infinite Energy: The Secret to Never Feeling Drained
Lightning Focus: Mastering the Art of Productivity in a Distracted World
Saturnalia Manifestation Magick: A Guide to Unlocking Abundance During the Solstice
Graboids and Garland: The Ultimate Tremors-Themed Christmas Guide
12 Nights of Holiday Magic
The Power of Pause: 60-Second Mindfulness Practices

The Quick Reset: How to Reclaim Your Life After Burnout

The Shadow Eater: A Tale of Despair and Survival

The Micro-Mastery Method: Transform Your Skills in Just Minutes a Day

Reclaiming Time: How to Live More by Doing Less

Chronovore: The Eternal Nexus

The Mind Reset: Unlocking Your Inner Peace in a Chaotic World

Confidence Code: Building Unshakable Self-Belief

Baby the Vampire Terrier

If you want solar for your home go here: https://www.harborsolar.live/apophisenterprises/

Get Some Tarot cards: https://www.makeplayingcards.com/sell/apophis-occult-shop

<u>**Get some shirts: https://www.bonfire.com/store/apophis-shirt-emporium/**</u>

**<u>Instagrams:</u>**
@apophis_enterprises,
@apophisbookemporium,
@apophisscardshop
Twitter: @apophisenterpr1
 Tiktok:@apophisenterprise
Youtube: @sg1fan23477, @FiresideRetreatKingdom
Hive: @sg1fan23477
CheeLee: @SG1fan23477

**Podcast: Apophis Chat Zone:** https://open.spotify.com/show/ 5zXbrCLEV2xzCp8ybrfHsk?si=fb4d4fdbdce44dec

**Newsletter:** https://apophiss-newsletter-27c897.beehiiv.com/

If you want to support me or see posts of other projects that I have come over to: **<u>buymeacoffee.com/mpetchinskg</u>**

I post there daily several times a day

Get your Dinowicca or Christmas themed digital products, especially Santa Raptor songs and other musics. Here: **https://sg1fan23477.gumroad.com**

Apophis Yuletide Digital has not only digital Christmas items, but it will have all things with Dinowicca as well as other Digital products.